Sweater started reading the letter.

Dear Sweater,

I'm writing to you on this day of

wet weather to say that this

letter is really

for your sister, Heather.

I like her.

Do you think she likes me?

If you would, Sir, could you please have

her circle 'NO'....or.... 'Yes', Sir?

Although I have only ever met her once,

each day I think of her

it makes me feel better.

I will never forget her and what she

did that day---

that day that Heather found and

gave me an eagle's feather.

And maybe someday

we'll be together.

But Sweater,

remember....

you and I will stay best friends forever.

After Sweater finished reading Clyde's tender letter, he looked at the envelope made of finished leather and thought to himself...

"Clyde sure is clever!!"

And smiling, he said,

"Clyde, I'll be sure Heather receives your

incredible letter."

"I hope you two end up

together."

"And count on you and I staying

best friends...

Forever."

THE END.

Made in the USA
Monee, IL
24 August 2020